IT'S HARD TO B[E A] VERB!

Activity and Idea Book

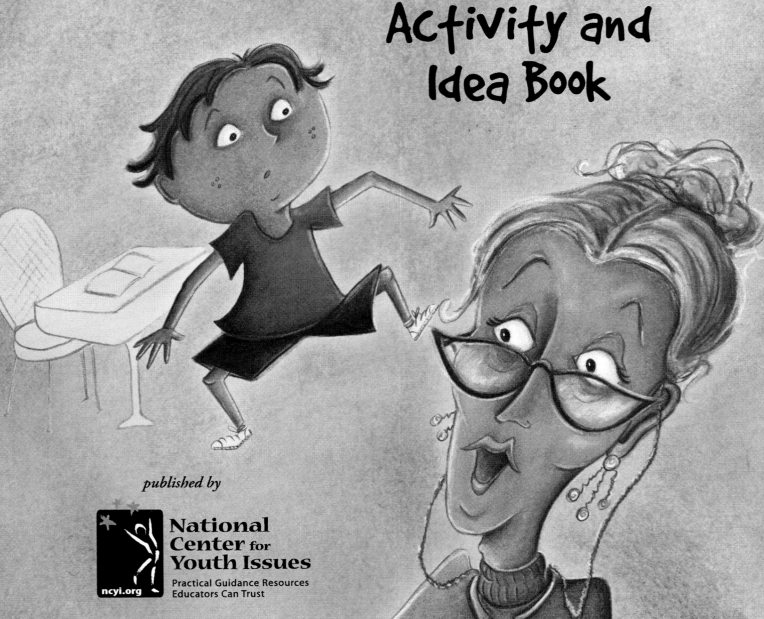

published by

National Center for Youth Issues
Practical Guidance Resources
Educators Can Trust

ncyi.org

A Note To Educators

My Mama always told me, "You get more bees with honey than you do vinegar!" When you are teaching a "VERB" or any child for that matter, this is always the case. Children who struggle with focus and organizational skills can be very frustrating to deal with, yet the more positive you can be with them, the better they will do in the classroom.

The purpose of this book is to offer teachers and ALL students "hands on" activities that can help them become more successful. When you are dealing with a "VERB," it is the little things that can make a big difference! External organization becomes vital for success both in and out of the classroom.

How to Teach a "VERB!" – A Quick Teacher Recipe

1. Stay Positive.
2. Be Organized.
3. Start each day with a clean slate.
4. Set reasonable expectations.
5. Work *with* the "VERB" as opposed to working *against* him/her.
6. Do everything you can to see the world from their perspective.

This book was especially fun for me to create because…I am a "VERB!"

ENJOY!

–Julia Cook

Duplication and Copyright

National Center for Youth Issues
Practical Guidance Resources
Educators Can Trust

ncyi.org

P.O. Box 22185
Chattanooga, TN 37422-2185
423.899.5714 • 866.318.6294
fax: 423.899.4547
www.ncyi.org
ISBN: 978-1-931636-55-1
© 2010 National Center for Youth Issues, Chattanooga, TN
All rights reserved.

Summary: A supplementary teacher's guide for *It's Hard To Be A Verb!*.
Full of discussion questions and exercises to share with students.

Written by: Julia Cook
Illustrations by: Carrie Hartman
Published by National Center for Youth Issues

Printed at Starkey Printing
Chattanooga, TN, USA
April 2016

My own Amazing work Shield!

When there is a lot going on in the classroom, "Verbs" have a tough time focusing on their own independent work. A work shield can help them focus by creating a distraction barrier.

Materials Needed
3 manilla folders
Stapler
Markers or Crayons

1. Staple the manilla folders together so they create a three-sided shield (see illustration).

2. Have students decorate one side of the folders any way they like. The student can even write, "My OWN AMAZING WORK SHIELD!" on the folders.

3. Have students brainstorm and write down three personal work goals on a sheet of paper. Goals might include: I will focus on the work I need to do. I will complete my work to the best of my ability. I will stay in my seat during work time, etc.

4. Have students copy their goals on the other side of the folders so that when they are working, they can look at their personal goals, but not be distracted by their fantastic work shield designs.

5. When it is time for independent seat work, have students set up their shields on their desks. Shields can easily be folded and stored inside their desks when not in use.

focus Squishy Basket

Fill a basket full of small items that can be used as focus squishies. Items can include: stress balls, three pieces of swing set chain hooked together, small soft toys, bendable plastic coated toys, silly putty, etc. Make sure you have twice as many focus squishies as you have students. (This will lessen their importance because everyone can have them when they need them.)

Explain to your students that some kids can listen more effectively if their fingers are busy moving. Tell your students, "The purpose of the focus squishy is to add to your learning NOT take away from it." Allow students to choose a focus squishy for the day. They can keep it on their desks, and when they need to listen actively, they can use it to keep their fingers busy. The focus squishies are NOT to be used as toys. They have a very important job to do and must be treated with respect!!! When they are not needed, they are to be placed carefully on top of the student's desk. Having a focus squishy and using it correctly can do wonderful things for your brain!!!

At the end of the day, have students clean their focus squishy with hand sanitizer and put it back in the basket. They can then be "squished" by others who are focusing the very next day.

The Sounds of a Learning Classroom!

When working with children who have ADD and ADHD, research has proven that the more natural and open a person feels in their surroundings, the more their symptoms of distractibility and hyperactivity will improve. During work time, fill your classroom with the sounds of nature by playing CDs with ocean waves, blowing trees, chirping birds, waterfalls etc.

Rock and Roll Your Wiggles!

Create a CD containing several fast paced, kid-appropriate songs. You can use rock and roll, oldies, hip hop, fast country, and/or jock jams.

Whenever your students seem to be a bit too wiggly, stop what you are doing and put on a song. Play it as loud as you can (make sure you don't disturb other classrooms.) Have your students stand up and wiggle to the music!

Terrific Tips for Teaching Verbs

1. Keeping a positive attitude is an absolute MUST! Be an "I can" teacher instead of an "I can't teacher. Do everything that you can do to convince your students that they are "I can" students instead of "I can't" students.

2. Create a secret sign with your "verb" (i.e. a hand on their shoulder etc.) that reminds them that they are off task without calling negative attention to them from you or from other students.

3. Have realistic expectations for each child, not one blanket expectation for your entire class.

4. Break up work time into shorter segments for your "verbs" to accommodate their excess energy. Allow them to get up and move around, stretch, get a drink, run an errand etc. in the middle of work time. Hold high expectations that when given a short break, the student will return to their assignments and be productive.

5. Play nature sound CDs (ocean waves, trees blowing, waterfall noise, birds chirping, etc.) softly in your classroom during work time. Get kids outside for fresh air whenever possible, even if it is just for 2 minutes!

6. Prior to work time, do the wiggle dance, or other physical activity that will get your students' blood flowing to their brains.

7. Start each day with a clean slate. Each day should be filled with a sense of hope for a successful day - both from the teacher and from the student.

8. Provide immediate feedback and give reinforcements whenever you see improvement. Reward success in every way possible!

9. Establish control by being consistent with classroom rules and boundaries. Discipline offenses immediately (most "verbs" function best in the "NOW.") Offer explanations when rules are violated. Be willing to actively listen to their side of the story, and then brainstorm together a positive alternative for future use.

10. Utilize group work. Encourage problem solving, teamwork and cooperation.

11. Use teaching visuals whenever possible and try to involve as many senses as you can in your direct teaching (i.e. see, smell, hear, taste, feel, etc.).

What can You Make of It?

How many words (two or more letters) can you make from the phrase:
IT'S HARD TO BE A VERB!

Write your answers below. Use the back of the paper if you run out of room.

1. _____

2. _____

3. _____

4. _____

5. _____

6. _____

7. _____

8. _____

9. _____

10. _____

11. _____

12. _____

13. _____

14. _____

15. _____

16. _____

17. _____

18. _____

19. _____

20. _____

21. _____

22. _____

Think About It (Being a Verb!)

Sometimes, it's FUN to be a "verb".

Write down five fun things you *like* about being a "verb":

1. _____
2. _____
3. _____
4. _____
5. _____

Circle one of the five FUN things. Write about a time when you *enjoyed* being a "verb".
Briefly explain what happened and how you felt about your actions.

_____

_____

_____

Sometimes, it's NOT-SO-FUN to be a "verb".

Write down five not-so-fun things you *don't like* about being a "verb":

1. _____
2. _____
3. _____
4. _____
5. _____

Circle one of the five NOT-SO-FUN things. Write about a time when you *didn't enjoy* being a "verb".
Briefly explain what happened and how you felt about your actions.

_____

_____

_____

What could you have done differently that would have made the situation better for you?

_____

_____

_____

Think About It (Living with a Verb!)

Sometimes, people think it's FUN to be around a "verb".

Write down five fun things others *like* about you being a "verb":

1. _____
2. _____
3. _____
4. _____
5. _____

Circle one of the five FUN things. Write about a time when others *enjoyed* you being a "verb". Briefly explain what happened and how they felt about your actions.

_____

_____

_____

Sometimes, people think it's NOT-SO-FUN to be around a "verb".

Write down five not-so-fun things others *don't like* about you being a "verb":

1. _____
2. _____
3. _____
4. _____
5. _____

Circle one of the five NOT-SO-FUN things. Write about a time when others *didn't enjoy* you being a "verb". Briefly explain what happened and how they felt about your actions.

_____

_____

_____

What could you have done differently that would have made the situation better for them?

_____

_____

_____

Campaign for VERBS!

Directions:

You are in the VERB promotion business.
Think of a catchy phrase that can be used to promote "verbs"
and design a t-shirt using your phrase.

"Verbs" help
to color our
world!

Picture This

Draw a picture of a "verb" when he's *in control* of his actions.

10

Daily Notebook Checklist

- Have students label the top of the pages with the days and dates of school one week at a time.

- Each morning, have students create a to-do check list and activity times for that day on each designated sheet of notepaper.

- Let them keep the notebook on their desks throughout the day and check off their daily tasks/activities as they do them.

- When deadlines are approaching, have students list the deadlines in their notebooks as announced. Have them write deadline reminders throughout the notebook as well.

- These notebooks are to remain at school and are not to be taken home at night. Students can copy off information from the notebook into a planner as needed.

- The notebook ends up being a great record of all that took place throughout the year.

Another idea

- Copy the following calendar template for each child. Have students fill in the numbers correctly and put the name of the month at the top of the page.

- Each morning, write the daily schedule along with times on the board for your students to copy onto their calendar. When important deadlines are announced, have them also record them on their calendars.

Note To Teachers

To some "verbs," the daily schedule that is written on the board is too abstract to apply. When "verbs" have their own personal copy of the daily schedule sitting on their desks, it becomes much easier for them to keep track of what is going on.

Three Little Monkeys

Try to find a visual or picture to represent "Hear No Evil, See No Evil, Speak No Evil." Often, if you look at a knick knack shop, you can find a figurine of the three monkeys that represent this famous quote. Within your classroom, transfer the meaning of this symbol into:

Hear the Lesson!   See the Lesson!   Speak the Lesson!

After your direct teaching (which should not last longer than about 10 minutes,) ask three students to come forward. Have one student write down on the chalkboard what they have heard you say. Ask the second student to show the class what they have seen you do. Have the third student be the teacher and quickly re-teach the lesson to the class.

Math On A Roll!

Divide your class into teams of four and give each team a large piece of roll paper (bulletin board covering) and a marker. Have them write all of their names at the top of the paper and do their math assignment with the big marker on the paper. The marker should rotate through all four team members. When a student is not doing the problem, their job is to watch over the student who has the marker, make sure they write the problem down correctly, and make sure they do the problem correctly. Whatever score the large paper gets on the assignment will be the individual score for each team member. "If you really know a skill, you can teach it to someone else." This exercise gives all students ("verbs" and "non-verbs") a chance to move, cooperate, learn, and teach each other.

It's Time for the Chime

Many "verbs" have problems with transition times. Having a wind chime in your room can signal a change in activity in a calming and tranquil manner. Simply rattle the chime when a transition time starts and students have until the chime settles to stop what they are doing and begin to focus on the next event.

What Part of Speech Are You??

Louis is a "verb"! He is super active and is always doing something.

What part of speech best describes you? _____

Why? _____

_____

Read Louis' poem from the book, "It's Hard To Be a Verb!" below.

> *My knees start itching. My toes start twitching.*
> *My skin gets jumpy. Others get grumpy.*
> *When it comes to sitting still, it's just not my deal.*
> *Haven't you heard…I am a VERB!*

Now write a poem about yourself using the part of speech that best describes you.

_____

_____

_____

_____

_____

_____

The Daily Classroom Journal

- Write down the days of the week on the end of wooden craft sticks and put them into a cup.

- At the beginning of each week have five students draw a stick from the cup.

- Write the names of the students on the board and their corresponding days next to their name.

- Each day, have that designated student create a journal entry explaining everything that went on throughout that day. Have them draw pictures or take digital pictures whenever possible. Allow the student who creates the daily entry to substitute the journal entry for one daily assignment.

- Place the journal pages inside plastic sleeves and put them in order in a 3 ring binder. The journal can serve as a great way to reflect upon your year. It can also help those who have been absent find out what they missed.

My 10 Minutes

Teachers have a lot of information to teach their students. Since "verbs" often struggle with listening skills during direct instruction times, try using the "My Ten Minutes" approach.

"I know that it is hard for you to sit and listen for long periods of time, so I am going to use the "My 10 Minutes" approach. Each time that I need you to really listen to what I have to say, I will ask you to give me ten minutes of your time. We will call this "My Ten Minutes."

"During 'My 10 Minutes,' I will need you to listen with your ears, your eyes, your whole entire body!!! You will need to really focus! You cannot talk or ask questions during 'My Ten Minutes.' If I can't say what I need to say in ten minutes, then I will have to either borrow a few more minutes of your time, or talk to you another time."

When "verb"s realize that you are asking them to focus for just ten minutes instead of an entire day, they will usually put forth a bit more effort. Please do not exceed your ten minutes unless you ask your students for more time. If you can't say what you need to say in 10 focused minutes, you may be saying too much.

The Top Secret Cylinder
NEVER LOSE IMPORTANT PAPERS AGAIN!!!!!!

TOP-SECRET

Have each child bring an empty potato chip can to school. Cover each can with white paper and allow the students to decorate their cans with markers, crayons, stickers etc.

Tell your students that this can is their Top-Secret Cylinder. Its job is to hold all of the important notes and papers that need to travel between home and school. The TSC is to stay in their back pack at all times unless being loaded and unloaded.

The Verb Villa

"Verbs" often get distracted during classroom work time. Designate a desk in a quiet part of your classroom calling it the "Verb Villa." Encourage kids to move to that desk if they are having a difficult time completing tasks. The Verb Villa is NOT to be viewed as a punishment, it needs to be used as an opportunity that any child can take advantage of.

A Blizzard of Compliments

Pass out an empty sheet of white paper to each student. Have them write down three generic compliments that they would like to hear other people give them: i.e. – You are a great friend! You are fun to hang out with. Etc.

Divide your class into two teams, and move all of your desks to the outer edges of your classroom so that you have a large open space in the center.

Have each team stand on opposite sides of the room and face each other.

Have each student tightly wad up their paper into a paper snowball.

Start playing some fun, bouncy background music, and as long as the music is playing, have the students throw their snowballs across the room at each other over and over and over again until all of the snow balls are mixed up.

Periodically stop the music and have each child grab a random snowball, open it up and read it to him/herself.

Restart the music and have the kids wad up the paper in their hands and start throwing snowballs again.

Do this continuously for up to 3 minutes depending on how much time and energy your kids have.

Having a snowball fight is a great way to share some compliments, build one another's self-esteem, and get your verbie wiggles out.

It is also a lot of fun!

You Do The "Wiggle Dance!"

Louis' mom taught him how to do the wiggle dance. It goes like this:

> *Scratch your knees.*
> *Wiggle your toes.*
> *Stretch your skin.*
> *Crinkle your nose.*
> *Shake your elbows.*
> *Bend at the waist*
> *Dance in a circle and*
> *Scrunch up your face!*

• Divide your classroom up into teams of four (some groups may be made up of three if needed.)

• Give each team 10-15 minutes to practice doing their version of the wiggle dance. They can use Louis' mom's words, or come up with a version of their own.

• Have each group perform their wiggle dance for the rest of the class.

Extension: Allow each group to choreograph their wiggle dance to music and teach the entire class each dance. As a class, practice doing a different dance each day whenever they need to get their wiggles out. Have the creators for each dance lead the class when their dance is chosen.

The Chain Of Good Deeds!

Cut out strips of multi-colored paper that can be used to make a paper chain. Create and decorate a sign that says: The Chain of Good Deeds! Each time you see one of your students do something that might fall into the category of a "good deed," give them a paper strip and have them write their name on the strip and what they did to earn it. Attach the strip as a link on the chain. How many links will you have by the end of the year???

Puzzle Mania

Jigsaw puzzles are a great way to promote inductive and deductive reasoning skills. They also provide students with a "hands on" way of working together to achieve a common goal. Often, the "verbs" in our classrooms are fidgety. When used appropriately, jigsaw puzzles can offer fidgety fingers a quiet, yet productive outlet.

- Set up a very large jigsaw puzzle (500-1500 pieces depending on the age of your students) on a card table in the back of your classroom.

- Allow students to work on the puzzle for short periods of time throughout the day, either individually or in small groups of two or three.

- Explain to your students that if one person had to complete this big puzzle all by themselves, it would take them a very long time, but by working together as a class, it shouldn't take too long at all.

- If a "verb" is struggling with staying on task during work time, allow him/her to take a quick break and go work at the puzzle table. Make sure the quick break is structured with a specific time limit (i.e. 5-7 min) and is followed with a promise to resume their classroom work immediately after the break.

- You can also use the puzzle table as a reward for completing an assignment.

- When the puzzle is completed, you may want to glue it together and display it in your classroom. Then start on another puzzle. At the end of the school year, celebrate your cooperative accomplishments and then raffle the glued puzzles off to your students.

Show it off!!

Materials Need:
Wax Paper • 1 Bottle of Mod Podge

1. Carefully place the finished jigsaw puzzle on a sheet of wax paper. Wax paper is the easiest surface on which to glue the finished puzzle. Wax paper won't peel the backing off of the puzzle like newspaper or cardboard will.
2. Next dip your brush into the bottle of Mod Podge and apply an even coat of the glue onto the jigsaw puzzle. Apply the brush strokes in the same direction. The glue goes on white, but dries clear. It usually is not necessary to apply another coat to the puzzle if the first coat seemed to hold it nicely together.
3. The jigsaw puzzle should be dry within the hour. Carefully peel off the wax paper and the puzzle is now ready for framing.

Verb in a Bag!

A great activity for all learners, especially the wiggly ones!!!

- Have each child write down a list of 10 "verbs" on 10 different strips of paper.

- Divide your class into two teams and give each team a small paper brown bag.

- Have each child put their "verb" strips into their team bag and shake up the bag to mix up the "verbs".

- Give Team One's bag to Team Two and vice versa.

- Have three members of Team One come to the front of the room and tell one of them to draw a "verb" strip out of their bag (containing "verbs" from Team Two.)

- They have 15 seconds to decide what to do and up to one minute to perform their "verb" for their team.

- If their team can guess their "verb" within one minute, Team One gets a point. If they can't Team Two gets a point.

- Next, allow Team Two to do the same. Then repeat.

- The first team to reach 10 points wins!!! If both teams reach 10 points at the same time while taking turns, have a play off until one team out scores another.

Kids Teaching Kids

- Split up any science or social studies chapter into concepts and/or main points.

  - Write the concepts/main points down on strips of small paper, number them in sequence, fold them up and place them in a jar.

  - Divide your class up into groups (2-4 kids) so that there are enough groups to cover each concept.

  - Have a student from each draw a concept from the jar.

  - Have each group work together to develop a lesson plan to teach their concept to the rest of the class. Encourage them to use outside resources, visual props, sound effects, etc. – whatever it takes to make a lasting impression. Allow appropriate time to work on and practice their lesson plans.

  - Have each group take turns presenting their lessons to the rest of the class. While each group presents, have the non-presenting students take notes and allow them a time to ask the presenting group questions.

  - Allowing your students to obtain ownership in what they are learning can make a huge difference in what they can retain. Remember "If you really know a subject well, you can teach it to someone else!"

Time to color

Staying Above the Line

"Verbs" often don't realize when they are off task or when their actions are inappropriate. "Staying Above The Line" is a great way to help all students become more aware of their actions.

Instructions

Draw a line on your chalkboard.

Explain to students that in order to stay above the line, a person needs to make good choices. When bad choices are made, this causes students to fall below the line. Brainstorm with students actions and words that will put them both above and below the line. (i.e. working quietly and independently, helping others, following direction ABOVE - Talking out, getting out of your seat at the wrong time, being disruptive to another classmate, giving a put-down etc - BELOW)

Draw a line across your bulletin board.

Allow each student to decorate a 3"x 5" card with their name on it using markers and stickers etc. Each morning have your student name cards stuck to the board with ticky tack two to three inches above the line. When students do amazing things, move their name card higher above the line. When students make poor choices, move their name cards lower toward the line and at times even below the line. As soon as the behavior is being corrected move the name card back up on or near the line. This serves as a great visual reminder to kids when their "Verbiness" starts to shine through in undesirable ways.

Keep this activity as positive as possible. When a kid moves up, be verbal about it and compliment them. When you have to pull a kid down below the line, do *not* be verbal. Your actions will speak louder than your words. Make sure that each morning all of your name cards start out above the line because each day is a new day, and everyone should start out with a clean slate and above the line (start them out where you want them to stay- Above The Line!).

Hint: Sometimes it works very well to have students be responsible for moving their own cards above and below the line.

Focus Bingo

Have students cut out the squares and paste them to their Bingo Cards (next page) in any order they wish (make sure they don't cover up the free-space.) Each child will have 5 extra squares so they can pick and choose a bit as to what they want on their card.

Whenever you see a student doing something positive that is on the Focus Bingo master list, give that student a sticker. Award prizes for Bingo winners and allow them to make a new card as soon as they win. If they get a sticker for something they have not chosen to put on their card, they may save it for their next Bingo card.

TEACHER: 5 of the squares above have been left blank so that you can write in your own personalized Bingo Spots.

I made it to school on time.	My work is turned in on time.	I spoke with good purpose.	I made great use of my time.	I made another person feel happy.
I waited patiently for my turn.	I walked quietly in the hall.	I DID NOT interrupt.	I did an amazing job on my assignment.	I helped a classmate with their work.
I did something to make my school a better place.	I kept my desk and/or work area clean.	I said "PLEASE" without being asked.	I said "THANK YOU" without being asked.	I followed instructions the first time.
I kept our classroom clean.	I brought back a note from home.	I was respectful to others.	I took a positive risk.	I cleaned up after myself.
I kept myself safe from injury at school.	I showed pride for my school.	I am a good problem solver.	I included someone who was feeling left out.	I shared with others.

A great way to reward kids for doing what's right!!

		FREE!		

More Than Words

Our author wants you to be her new illustrator.

In each box, draw a picture that goes with the words
from the story, *It's Hard To Be A Verb!*

*At school, we have to sit in our desks during work time. Work time lasts for 30 minutes.
To me, it seems like it lasts for 16 years! It's hard for me to stay at my desk.*

*I wiggled my wiggles before story time and they didn't end up wiggling me.
And, I used my Focus Squishy without anyone knowing about it and...
I got a STAR for being a good listener.*

Verb Games

Directions

- Pass out a small brown lunch sack to each student.
- Have students take the bag home and create a 15 minute activity that will fit inside the bag. Ask them to decorate the outside of the bag without revealing what is inside and to make sure all of the materials needed to do the activity are inside of the bag (including the instructions.)
- Staple the bags shut and bring them to school.

Examples may include

- **Build a mobile out of straws, twisty ties, string and paper.**
- **Build a spaceship using small gumdrops and toothpicks.**
- **Color a detailed design with markers or colored pencils.**
- **Make a self portrait with google eyes, yarn for hair, licorice strings for lips etc.**
- **Fold a fleet of paper airplanes and decorate them.**

Teachers

Place all of the bags on a table in your room. Whenever you need to take a brain break, at the end of a unit or grading period, have every student choose a bag besides the one they brought back to school. Have them open the bag and complete the activity inside. When they're finished, go around the room and have them explain what they did. Then find out who brought that activity and see if it was completed successfully. Have students then place all unused materials back inside the bag and return it to the person who created the activity. You may need to create a few extra bags to have on hand just in case some of your students are unable to create a bag.